John Habberton

Who was Paul Grayson?

John Habberton

Who was Paul Grayson?

ISBN/EAN: 9783337276119

Printed in Europe, USA, Canada, Australia, Japan

Cover: Foto ©Raphael Reischuk / pixelio.de

More available books at **www.hansebooks.com**

WHO WAS PAUL GRAYSON?

BY

JOHN HABBERTON
AUTHOR OF " HELEN'S BABIES " ETC.

ILLUSTRATED

NEW YORK

HARPER & BROTHERS, FRANKLIN SQUARE

1881

CONTENTS.

Contents.

ILLUSTRATIONS.

WHO WAS PAUL GRAYSON?

CHAPTER I.

THE NEW PUPIL.

IIE boys who attended Mr. Morton's Select
School in the village of Laketon did not pro-
fess to know more than boys of the same age
and advantages elsewhere; but of one thing they
were absolutely certain, and that was that no teacher ever rang his bell to assemble the school or call
the boys in from recess until just that particular instant when the fun in the school-yard was at its
highest, and the boys least wanted to come in. A
teacher might be very fair about some things: he
might help a boy through a hard lesson, or give him
fewer bad marks than he had earned; he might even

forget to report to a boy's parents all the cases of truancy in which their son had indulged; but when a teacher once laid his hand upon that dreadful bell and stepped to the window, it really seemed as if every particle of human sympathy went out of him.

On one bright May morning, however, the boys who made this regular daily complaint were few; indeed, all of them, except Bert Sharp, who had three consecutive absences to explain, and no written excuse from his father to help him out, were already inside the school-room, and even Bert stood where he could look through the open door while he cudgelled his wits and smothered his conscience in the endeavor to frame an explanation that might seem plausible. The boys already inside lounged near any desks but their own, and conversed in low tones about almost everything except the subject uppermost in their minds, this subject being a handsome but rather sober-looking boy of about fourteen years, who was seated at a desk in the back part of the room, and trying, without any success whatever, to look as if he did not know that all the other boys were looking at him.

It was not at all wonderful that the boys stared, for none of them had ever before seen the new pupil, and Laketon was so small a town that the appearance of a strange boy was almost as unusual an event as the coming of a circus.

"Let's give it up," said Will Palmer, who had for five minutes been discussing with several other boys all sorts of improbabilities about the origin of the new pupil; "let's give it up until roll-call; then we'll learn his name, and that 'll be a little comfort."

"I wish Mr. Morton would hurry, then," said Benny Mallow. "I came early this morning to see if I couldn't win back my striped alley from Ned Johnston, and this business has kept us from playing a single game. Quick, boys, quick! Mr. Morton's getting ready to touch the bell."

The group separated in an instant, and every member was seated before the bell struck; so were most of the other boys, and so many pairs of eyes looked inquiringly at the teacher that Mr. Morton himself had to bite his lower lip very hard to keep from laughing as he formally rang the school to order. As the roll was called, the boys answered to their names in a prompt, sharp, business-like way, quite unusual in school-rooms; and as the call proceeded, the responses became so quick as to sometimes get a little ahead of the names that the boys knew were coming.

Suddenly, as the names beginning with G were reached, and Charlie Gunter had his mouth wide open, ready to say "Here," the teacher called, "Paul Grayson."

"Here!" answered the new boy.

A slight sensation ran through the school; no boy did anything for which he had to be called to order, yet somehow the turning of heads, the catching of breath, and the letting go of breath that had been held in longer than usual, made a slight commotion, which reached the ears of the strange pupil, and made him look rather more ill at ease than before.

PAUL GRAYSON.

The answers to the roll became at once less spirited; indeed, Benny Mallow was staring so hard, now that he had a name to increase his interest in the stranger, that he forgot entirely to answer to his name, and was compelled to sit on the chair beside the teacher's desk from that moment until recess.

That recess seemed longer in coming than any other that the school had ever known—longer even than that memorable one in which a strolling trio of Italian musicians had been specially contracted with to begin playing in the school-yard the moment the boys came down. Finally, however, the bell rang half-past ten, and the whole roomful hurried downstairs, but not before Mr. Morton had called Joe Appleby, the largest boy in school, and formally introduced Paul Grayson, with the expressed wish that he should make his new companion feel at home among the boys.

Appleby went about his work with an air that showed how fully he realized the importance of his position: he introduced Grayson to every boy, beginning with the largest; and it was in vain that Benny Mallow, who was the youngest of the party, made all sorts of excuses to throw himself in the way of the distinguished couple, even to the extent of once getting his feet badly mixed up with those of Grayson. When, however, the ceremony ended, and Appleby was at liberty, so many of the boys crowded around him that the new pupil was in some danger of being lonely.

"Find out for yourselves," was Appleby's dignified reply to his questioners. "I don't consider it gentlemanly to tell everything I know about a man."

At this rebuke the smaller boys considered Appleby a bigger man than ever before, but some of the larger ones hinted that Appleby couldn't very well tell what he didn't know, at which Appleby took offence, and joined the group of boys who were leaning against a fence, in the shade of which Will Palmer had already inveigled the new boy into conversation.

"By-the-way," said Will, "there's time yet for a game or two of ball. Will you play?"

" Yes, I'll be glad to," said Grayson.

"Who else?" asked Will.

"I!" shouted all of the boys, who did not forget their grammar so far as to say " Me !" instead. Really, the eagerness of the boys to play ball had never be-fore been equalled in the memory of any one present, and Will Palmer cooled off some quite warm friends by his inability to choose more than two boys to complete the quartette for a common game of ball. It did the disappointed boys a great deal of good to hear the teacher's bell ring just as Will Palmer "caught himself in " to Grayson's bat.

"You play a splendid game," said Will to Gray-son, as they went up-stairs side by side. "Where did you learn it?"

Joe Appleby, who was on the step in front of the couple, dragged just an instant in order to catch the expected information, but all he got was a bump from Palmer that nearly tumbled him forward on his dignified nose, as Grayson answered,

"Oh, in several places; nowhere in particular."

Palmer immediately determined that he would follow his new schoolmate home at noon, and discover where he lived. Then he would interview the neighbors, and try to get some information ahead of that stuck-up Joe Appleby, who, considering he was only four months older than Palmer himself, put on too many airs for anything. But when school was dismissed, Palmer was disgusted at noting that at least half of the other boys were distributing themselves for just such an operation as the one he had planned. Besides, Grayson did not come down-stairs with the crowd. Could it be possible that he was from the country, and had brought a cold lunch to school with him? Palmer hurried up the stairs to see, but met the teacher and the new boy coming down, and the two walked away, and together entered the house of old Mrs. Bartle, where Mr. Morton boarded.

"He's a boarding scholar," exclaimed Benny Mallow. "I've read of such things in books."

"Then he'll be stuck up," declared Joe Appleby.

This opinion was delivered with a shake of the head that seemed to intimate that Joe had known all the ways of boarding - scholars for thousands of years; so most of the boys looked quite sober for a moment or two. Finally Sam Wardwell, whose father kept a store, broke the silence by remarking, "I'll bet he's from Boston; his coat is of just the same stuff as one that a drummer wears who comes to see father sometimes."

"Umph!" grunted Appleby; "do you suppose Boston has some kinds of cloth all to itself? *You* don't know much."

The smaller boys seemed to side with the senior pupil in this opinion; so Sam felt very uncomfortable, and vowed silently that he would bring a piece of chalk to school that very afternoon, and do some rapid sketching on the back of Appleby's own coat. Then Benny Mallow said: "Say, boys, this old school must be a pretty good one, after all, if people some-where else send boarders to it. His folks must be rich: did you notice what a splendid knife he cut

his finger-nails with?—'twas a four-blader, with a
pearl handle. But of course you didn't see it, and
I did; he used it in school, and my desk is right beside his."

Will Palmer immediately led Benny aside, and
offered him a young fan-tail pigeon, when his long-
expected brood was hatched, to change desks, if the
teacher's permission could be obtained. Meanwhile
Napoleon Nott, who generally was called Notty, and
who had more imagination than all the rest of the
boys combined, remarked, "I believe he's a foreign
prince in disguise."

"He's well-bred, anyhow," said Will Palmer to
Benny Mallow. "I hope he'll be man enough to
stand no nonsense. He's big enough, and smart
enough, if looks go for anything, to run this school,
and I'd like to see him do it—anything to get rid of
Joe Appleby's airs."

Then the various groups separated, moved by the
appetites that boys in good health always have.
One boy, however—Joe Appleby—was man enough

to deny his palate when greater interests devolved upon him, so he made some excuse to go back to the school-room, so as to be there when the teacher and his new charge returned. Half an hour later Benny Mallow, who had sneaked away from home as soon as the dessert had been brought in, and had vulgarly eaten his pie as he walked along the street—Benny Mallow walked into the school-room, and beheld the teacher, Joe Appleby, and Paul Grayson standing to-gether as if they had been talking. As Benny went to his seat Joe followed him, and bestowed upon him a look of such superiority that Benny deter-mined at once that some marvellous mystery must have been revealed, and that Joe was the custodian of the entire thing. Benny was so full of this fancy that he slipped down - stairs and told it as fact to each boy who appeared, the result being to make Joe Appleby a greater man than ever in the eyes of the school, while Grayson became a tormenting yet most invaluable mystery.

CHAPTER II.

THE FIGHT.

HE afternoon session of Mr. Morton's Select School was but little more promising of revelations about the new boy than the morning had been. Most of the boys returned earlier than usual from their respective dinners, and either hung about the school-room, staring at their new companion, or waited at the foot of the stairs for him to come down. The attentions of the first-named division soon became so distasteful to the new-comer that he left the room abruptly, and went down the stairway two steps at a time. At the door he found little Benny Mallow looking up admiringly, and determining to practice that particular method of coming down-stairs the first Saturday that he could creep unnoticed through a school-room window. But Benny was not one of those foolish boys who forget the present while planning about the future. Paul Grayson had barely reached the bottom step when little Benny looked innocently up into his face, and remarked, "Say!"

"Well?" Paul answered.

"You're the biggest boy in school," continued Benny. "I noticed it when you stood beside Appleby."

Grayson looked as if he did not exactly see that the matter was worthy of special remark.

"I," said Benny, "am the smallest boy—I am, really. If you don't believe it, look at the other boys. I'll just run down the steps, and stand beside some of them."

"Don't take that trouble," said Grayson, pleasantly. "But what is there remarkable about my height and your shortness?" ·

"Oh, nothing," said Benny, looking down with some embarrassment, and then looking up again—

"only I thought maybe 'twas a good reason why we should be friends."

"Why, so it is, little fellow," said Grayson. "I was very stupid not to understand that without being told."

"All right, then," said Benny, evidently much relieved in mind. "Anything you want to know I'll tell you—anything that I know myself, that is. Because I'm little, you mustn't think I don't know everything about this town, because I do. I know where you can fish for bass in a place that no other boy knows anything about: what do you think of that? I know a big black-walnut tree that no other boy ever saw ; of course there's no nuts on it now, but you can see last year's husks if you like. Have you got a sister?"

Grayson suddenly looked quite sober, and answered, "No."

"I have," said Benny, "and she is the nicest girl in town. If you want to know some of the bigger girls, I suppose you'll have to ask Appleby. What's

the use of big girls, though? They never play marbles with a fellow, or have anything to trade. Say
—I hope *you're* not too big to play marbles?"

"Oh no," said Grayson; "I'll buy some, and we'll
have a royal game."

"Don't do it," said Benny; "I've got a pocketful.
Come on." And to the great disgust of all the
larger boys Benny led his new friend into the school-
yard, scratched a ring on the dirt, divided his stock
of marbles into two equal portions, and gave one to
Grayson; then both boys settled themselves at a
most exciting game, while all the others looked on
in wonder, with which considerable envy and jeal-
ousy were mixed up.

"That Benny Mallow is putting on more airs than
so little a fellow can carry; don't you think so?"
said Sam Wardwell to Ned Johnston.

"I should say so," was the reply; "and that isn't
all. The new fellow isn't going to be thought much
of in this school if he's going to allow himself to be-
long to any youngster that chooses to take hold of

him. I'll tell you one thing: Joe Appleby's birthday party is to come off in a few days, and I'll bet
you a fish-line to a button that Master Benny won't
get near enough to it to smell the ice-cream. How
will that make the little upstart feel?"

"Awful—perfectly awful," said Sam, who, being
very fond of ice-cream himself, could not imagine a
more terrible revenge than Ned had suggested. Just
then Bert Sharp sauntered up with his hands in his
pockets, his head craned forward as usual, and his
eyes trying to get along faster than his head.

"See here," said he, "if that new boy boards with
the teacher, he's going to tell everything he knows.
I think somebody ought to let him know what he'll
get if he tries that little game. I'm not going to
be told on: I have a rough enough time of it now."
Bert spoke feelingly, for he was that afternoon to
remain at school until he had recited from memory
four pages of history, as a punishment for his long
truancy.

"Who's going to tell him, though?" asked Sam.

JUST IN TIME TO SEE GRAYSON GIVE BENT A BLOW IN THE CHEST.

"It should be some fellow big enough to take care of himself, for Grayson looks as if he could be lively."

"I'll do it myself," declared Bert, savagely; saying which he lounged over toward the ring at which Benny and Grayson were playing. The boys had seen Bert in such a mood before, so at once there was some whispered cautions to look out for a fight. Before Bert had been a minute beside the ring, Grayson accidentally brushed against him as, half stooping, he followed his alley across the ring. Bert immediately got his hands out of his pockets, and struck Grayson a blow on the back of the neck that felled him to the ground. All the boys immediately rushed to the spot, but before they had reached it the new pupil was on his feet; and the teacher reached the window, bell in hand, just in time to see Grayson give Bert a blow on the chest that caused the young man to go reeling backward, and yell "Oh!" at the top of his voice. Then the bell rang violently, and all of the boys but Bert Sharp hurried up-stairs, Grayson not even taking the trouble to look behind him. In the scramble toward the seats Will Palmer found a chance to whisper to Ned Johnston, "There's no nonsense about him, eh?"

And Ned replied, " He's splendid!"

All of the boys seemed of Ned's opinion, for when Mr. Morton, just as Bert Sharp entered, rang the school to order, and asked, " Who began that fight?" there was a general reply of, " Bert Sharp."

"Sharp, Grayson, step to the front," commanded the teacher.

Bert shuffled forward with a very sullen face, while Grayson stalked up so bravely that Benny Mallow risked getting a mark by kicking Sam Wardwell's feet under the desk to attract his attention, and then whispering, " Just look at that!"

Before the teacher could speak to either of the two boys in front of him, Grayson said, " I'm very sorry, sir, but I was knocked down for nothing, unless it was brushing against him by mistake."

" Was that the cause, Sharp?" asked Mr. Morton.

Bert hung his head a little lower, which is a way

THE RECONCILIATION.

that all boys have when they are in the wrong; so the teacher did not question him any farther, but said:

"Boys, Grayson is a stranger here. I know him to be a boy of good habits and manners, and I give you my word that if you have any trouble with him, you will have to begin it yourselves. And if you expect to be gentlemen when you grow up, you must learn now to treat strangers as you would like to be treated if away from your own homes. Grayson, Sharp, go to your seats."

"May I speak to Sharp, sir?" asked Grayson.

"Yes," said Mr. Morton.

"I'm sorry I hit you," said the new boy. "Will you shake hands and be friends?"

Bert looked up suspiciously without raising his head, but Grayson's hand was outstretched, and as Bert did not know what else to do, he put out his own hand; and then the two late enemies returned to their seats, Bert looking less bad-tempered than usual, and Grayson looking quite sober.

Somehow at the afternoon recess every boy treated

Grayson as if he had known him for years, and no one seemed to be jealous when Grayson invited Bert to play marbles with him, and insisted on his late adversary taking the first shot. But the teacher's remarks about Grayson had only increased the curiosity of the boys about their new comrade, and when Sam Wardwell remarked that old Mrs. Bartle, with whom the teacher and his pupil boarded, bought groceries nearly every evening at his father's store, and he would just lounge about during the rest of the afternoon and ask her about Grayson when she came in, at least six other boys offered to sit on a board-pile near the store and wait for information.

As for Grayson, he sat in the school-room writing while the teacher waited, for more than an hour after the general dismissal, to hear Bert Sharp recite those detestable four pages of history, and Bert was a great deal slower at his task than he would have been if he had not had to wonder why Grayson had to do so much writing.

Chapter III.

MUSIC AND MANNERS.

HE boys at Mr. Morton's Select School were not the only people at Laketon who were curious about Paul Grayson. Although the men and women had daily duties like those of men and women elsewhere, they found a great deal of time in which to think and talk about other people and their affairs. So all the boys who attended the school were interrogated so often about their new comrade, that they finally came to consider themselves as being in some way a part of the mystery.

Mr. Morton, who had opened his school only several weeks before the appearance of Grayson, was himself unknown at Laketon until that spring, when, after an unsuccessful attempt to be made principal

of the grammar-school, he had hired the upper floor
of what once had been a store building, and opened
a school on his own account. He had introduced
himself by letters that the school trustees and Mr.
Merivale, pastor of one of the village churches, considered very good; but now that Grayson's appearance was explained only by the teacher's statement
that the boy was son of an old school friend who
was now a widower, some of the trustees wished they
were able to remember the names and addresses
appended to the letters that the new teacher had
presented. Sam Wardwell's father having learned
from Mr. Morton where last he had taught, went
so far as to write to the wholesale merchants with
whom he dealt, in New York, for the name of some
customer in Mr. Morton's former town; but even by
making the most of this roundabout method of in-
quiry he only learned that the teacher had been
highly respected, although nothing was known of his
antecedents.

With one of the town theories on the subject of

Mr. Morton and Paul Grayson the boys entirely dis-
agreed : this was that the teacher and the boy were
father and son.

"I don't think grown people are so very smart,
after all," said Sam Wardwell, one day, as the boys
who were not playing lounged in the shade of the
school - building and chatted. "They talk about
Grayson being Mr. Morton's son. Why, who ever
saw Grayson look a bit afraid of the teacher?"

"Nobody," replied Ned Johnston, and no one con-
tradicted him, although Bert Sharp suggested that
there were other boys in the world who were not
afraid of their fathers—himself for instance.

"Then you ought to be," said Benny Mallow.
Benny looked off at nothing in particular for a moment, and then continued, "I wish I had a father to
be afraid of."

There was a short silence after this, for as no other
boy in the group had lost a father, no one knew
exactly what to say; besides, a big tear began to
trickle down Benny's face, and all the boys saw it,

although Benny dropped his head as much as possible. Finally, however, Ned Johnston stealthily
patted Benny on the back, and then Sam Wardwell,
taking a fine winter apple from his pocket, broke it
in two, and extended half of it, with the remark,
"Halves, Benny."

Benny said, "Thank you," and seemed to take a
great deal of comfort out of that piece of apple, while
the other boys, who knew how fond Sam was of all
things good to eat, were so impressed by his gener-
osity that none of them asked for the core of the
half that Sam was stowing away for himself. Indeed, Ned Johnston was so affected that he at once
agreed to a barter—often proposed by Sam, and as
often declined—of his Centennial medal for a rather
old bass-line with a choice sinker.

Before the same hour of the next day, however,
nearly every boy who attended Mr. Morton's school
was wicked enough to wish to be in just exactly
Benny Mallow's position, so far as fathers were con-
cerned. This sudden change of feeling was not

caused by anything that Laketon fathers had done, but through fear of what they might do. As no two boys agreed upòn a statement of just how this difference of sentiment occurred, the author is obliged to tell the story in his own words.

Usually the boys hurried away from the neighborhood of the school as soon as possible after dismissal in the afternoon, but during the last recess of the day on which the above-recorded conversation occurred Will Palmer and Charley Gunter completed a series of a hundred games of marbles, and had the strange fortune to end exactly even. The match had already attracted a great deal of attention in the school—so much so that boys who took sides without thinking had foolishly made a great many bets on the result, and a deputation of these informed the players that it would be only the fair thing to play the deciding game that afternoon after school, so that boys who had bet part or all of their property might know how they stood. Will and Charley expressed no objection; indeed, each was so anx-

ious to prove himself the best player that in his anx-
iety he made many blunders during the afternoon
recitations.

As soon as the school was dismissed the boys hurried into the yard, while Grayson, who had lately
seen as much of marble-'playing as he cared to,
strolled off for a walk. The marble ring was
quickly scratched on the ground, and the players began work. But the boys did not take as
much interest in the game as they had expected to,
for a rival attraction had unexpectedly appeared
on the ground since recess; two rival attractions,
more properly speaking, or perhaps three, for in a
shady corner sat an organ-grinder, on the ground in
front of him was an organ, and on top of this sat
a monkey. Now to city boys more than ten years
of age an organ-grinder is almost as uninteresting
as a scolding; but Laketon was not a city, organ-
grinders reached it seldom, and monkeys less often;
so fully half the boys lounged up to within a few
feet of the strangers, and devoured them with their

eyes, while the man and the animal devoured some scraps of food that had been begged at a kitchen- door.

Nobody can deny that a monkey, even when so- berly eating his dinner, is a very comical animal, and no boy ever lived, not excepting that good little boy Abel, who did not naturally wonder what a strange animal would do if some one disturbed him in some way. Which of Mr. Morton's pupils first felt this wonder about the organ-grinder's monkey was never known; the boys soon became too sick of the gener- al subject to care to compare notes about this special phase of it; but the first one who ventured to ex- periment on the monkey was Bert Sharp, who made so skilful a "plumper" shot with a marble, from the level of his trousers pocket, that the marble struck the monkey fairly in the breast, and rat- tled down on the organ, while the monkey, who evidently had seen boys before, made a sudden jump to the head of his master, and then scrambled down the Italian's back, and hid himself so that

he showed only as much of his head as was necessary to his effort to peer across the organ-grinder's
shoulder.

"Maledetta!" growled the Italian, as he looked
inquiringly around him. As none of the boys had
ever before heard this word, they did not know
whether it was a question, a rebuke, or a threat; but
they saw plainly enough that the man was angry;
and although most of them stepped backward a pace
or two, they all joined in the general laugh that a
crowd of boys are almost sure to indulge in when
they see any one in trouble that any one of the
same boys would be sorry about were he alone
when he saw it.

The organ-grinder began munching his food very
rapidly, as if in haste to finish his meal, yet he did
not forget to pass morsels across his shoulder to his
funny little companion, and the manner in which
the monkey put up a paw to take the food amused
the boys greatly. Benny Mallow thought that
monkey was simply delightful, but he could not

help wondering what the animal would do if a
marble were to strike his paw as he put it up.
. Animals' paws are soft at bottom, reasoned Benny
to himself, and marbles shot through the air cannot hurt much, if any; the result of this short ar-
gument was that Benny tried a "plumper" shot
himself; but the marble, instead of striking the
monkey's paw, went straight into the mouth of
the organ-grinder, who was just about to take a
mouthful of bread.

Up sprung the Italian, with an expression of coun-
tenance so perfectly dreadful that Benny Mallow
dreamed of it, for a month after, whenever he ate
too much supper. All the boys ran, and the Italian
pursued them with words so strange and numerous
that the boys could not have repeated one of them
had they tried. Every boy was half a block away
before he thought to look around and see whether
the footsteps behind him were those of the organ-
grinder or of some frightened boy. Sam Wardwell
stumbled and fell, at which Ned Johnston, who had

been but a step or two behind, fell upon Sam, who instantly screamed, "Oh, don't, mister; I didn't do it—really I didn't."

On hearing this all the other boys thought it safe to stop and look, and when they saw the Italian was not in the street at all, they felt so ashamed that there is no knowing what they would have done if they had not had Sam Wardwell to laugh at. As for Sam, he was so angry about the mistake he had made that he vowed vengeance against the Italian, and hurried back toward the yard. Will Palmer afterward said that he couldn't see how the Italian was to blame, and Ned Johnston said the very same thought had occurred to him; but somehow neither of the two happened to mention the matter, as they, with the other boys, followed Sam Wardwell to see what he would do. Looking through the cracks of the fence, the boys saw the Italian, with his organ and monkey on his back, coming down the yard; at the same time they saw nearly half a brick go up the yard, and barely miss the organ-grinder's head. The man said nothing; perhaps he had been in difficulties with boys before, and had learned that the best way to get out of them was to walk away as fast as possible; besides, there was no one in sight for him to talk to, for Sam had started to run the instant that the piece of brick left his hand. The man came out of the yard, looked around, saw the boys, turned in the opposite direction, and then turned up an alley that passed one side of the school-house.

He could not have done worse; for no one lived on the alley, so any mischievous boy could tease him without fear of detection. He had gone but a few steps when Sam, who had hidden in a garden on the same alley, rose beside a fence, and threw a stick, which struck the organ. The man stopped, turned around, saw the whole crowd of boys slowly following, supposed some one of them was his assailant, threw the stick swiftly at the party, and then started to run. No one was hit, but the mere sight of a frightened man trying to escape seemed to rob the

boys of every particle of humanity. Charley Gunter, who was very fond of pets, devoted himself to
trying to hit the monkey with stones; Will Palmer, who had once helped nurse a friendless negro
who had cut himself badly with an axe, actually
shouted "Hurrah!" when a stone thrown by himself struck one of the man's legs, and made him
limp; Ned Johnston hurriedly broke a soft brick
into small pieces, and threw them almost in a
shower; and even Benny Mallow, who had always
been a most tender - hearted little fellow, threw
stones, sticks, and even an old bottle that he found
among the rubbish that had been thrown into the
alley.

Suddenly a stone—there were so many in the air
at a time that no one knew who threw that particular stone—struck the organ-grinder in the back of
the head, and the poor fellow fell forward flat, with
his organ on top of him, and remained perfectly mo-
tionless.

"He's killed!" exclaimed some one, as the pur-

ATTACK ON THE ORGAN-GRINDER.

suers stopped. In an instant all the boys went over the fences on either side of the alley, but not until Paul Grayson, crossing the upper end of the alley, had seen them, and they had seen him.

4

CHAPTER IV.

WHO WILL TELL?

S Benny Mallow hid himself in a barn in the yard into which he had jumped, he had only one distinct thought in his mind: he wished that the Italian had never come to Laketon at all—never come to the United States, in fact. He wished that the Italians had never heard of such a place as America: if one of the race had to discover it, he need not have gone and let his fellow - countrymen know all about it, so that they should come over with organs and monkeys, and get boys into trouble—boys that weren't doing a thing to that organ-grinder when he threw a stick at them. What made the fellow go into the school - yard, anyway? No one asked him to come. Now there would be a fuss made, of course; and if there was anything that Benny hated more than all other things, it was a fuss.

But what if the organ-grinder should really prove to be dead? Oh! that would be too dreadful; all the boys would have to be hanged, to be sure of punishing the murderer, just as the whole class was sometimes kept in for an hour because something wrong had been done, and no one would tell who did it.

Benny could not bear the thought of so dreadful a termination to his life, for he knew of a great deal worth living for; besides, his mother would need his help as soon as he grew old enough to earn anything. What should he do? Wait until dark, and then run away, and tramp off to the West, where other runaway boys went, or should he make for the sea-board, and from there to South America, from which country he had heard that criminals could not be brought back?

But first he ought to learn whether the man was really dead; it might not be necessary to run away

at all. But how should he find out? Suddenly he
remembered that Mr. Wardwell's barn, in which he
was, had a window opening on the alley; so he crept
up into the loft, and spent several moments in trying
to look up the alley without putting his head out
of the window. Finally, he partly hid his face by
holding a handful of hay in front of it, and peered
out. Between the stalks of hay he was delighted to
see the organ-grinder on his feet, although two men
were helping him. They were not both men, either,
Benny saw, after more careful looking, for one of
them was Paul Grayson; but the other—horror of
horrors!—was Mr. Stott, a justice of the peace. Benny knew that Justice Stott had sent many men to
jail for fighting, and if Grayson should tell who
took part in the attack, Benny had not the slightest doubt that half of Mr. Morton's pupils would be
sent to jail too.

This seemed more dreadful than the prospect of
being hanged had done, but it could be done more
quickly. Benny determined at once that he must

BENNY MALLOW IN THE BARN.

find out the worst, and be ready for it; so he waited until the injured man and his supporters had turned the corner of a street, and were out of sight; then he bounded into the alley again, hurried home, seized a basket that was lying beside the back door, and a moment later was sauntering along the street, whistling, and moving in a direction that seemed to be that in which he might manage to meet the three as if by accident. He did not take much comfort out of his whistling, for in his heart he felt himself to be the most shameful hypocrite that had existed since the days of Judas Iscariot, and the recollection of having been told by his Sunday-school teacher within a week that he was the best boy in his class seemed to make him feel worse instead of better; and his mind was not relieved of this unpleasant burden until at a shady corner he came suddenly upon the organ-grinder and his supporters, when he instantly exchanged his load for a new one.

"Why, what's the matter, Paul?" asked Benny,

with as much surprise in his tone and manner as he could affect.

Justice Stott had just gone into an adjacent yard for water for the Italian, when Grayson answered, with a very sober face, "You know as well as I do, Benny, and I saw the whole crowd."

"I don't!" exclaimed Benny, in all the despera-tion of cowardice. "I didn't do or see—"

"Sh — h!" whispered Grayson, "the Justice is coming back."

Benny turned abruptly and started for home. He felt certain that his face was telling tales, and that Justice Stott would learn the whole story if he saw him. There was one comfort, though: it was evident that Grayson did not want the Jus-tice to know that Benny had taken part in the affair.

There was a great deal of business transacted by the boys of Laketon that night. How it was all managed no one could have explained, but it is cer-tain that before bedtime every boy who had taken

part in the assault on the Italian knew that the
man was not dead, but had merely been stunned
and cut by a stone, and Paul Grayson knew who
were of the party that chased the man up the alley.
Various plans of getting out of trouble were in
turn suggested and abandoned; but several boys
for a long time insisted that the only chance of
safety lay in calling Grayson out of his boarding-
house, and threatening him with the worst whip-
ping that the boys, all working together, could give.
Even this idea was finally abandoned when Will
Palmer suggested that as Grayson boarded with
the teacher, and seemed to be in some sort a friend
of his, he probably would already have told all he
knew, if he was going to tell at all. Some consolation might have been got out of a report of Benny's short interview with Grayson, had Benny
thought to give it, but he had, on reaching home,
promptly feigned headache, and gone to bed; so
such of the boys as did not determine to play tru-
ant, and so postpone the evil day, thought bitterly

of the morrow as they dispersed to their several homes.

There was not as much playing as usual in the school-yard next morning; and when the class was summoned into school, the teacher had no difficulty in discovering, by the looks of the various boys, who were innocent and who guilty. Immediately after calling the roll Mr. Morton stood up and said:

"Boys, a great many of you know what I am going to talk about. Usually your deeds done out of school-hours are not for me to notice; but the cowardly, shameful treatment of that organ-grinder began in the school-yard, and before you had gone to your homes, so I think it my duty to inquire into the matter. Justice Stott thinks so too. When any one has done a wrong that he cannot amend, the only manly course is to confess. I want those boys who followed the organ-grinder up the alley to stand up."

No boy arose. Benny Mallow wished that some one would give the bottom of his seat a hard kick, so that he would have to rise in spite of himself, but no one kicked.

"Be honest, now," said Mr. Morton. "I have been a boy myself; I have taken part in just such tricks. I know how bad you feel, and how hard it is to confess; but I give you my word that you will feel a great deal better after telling the truth. I will give you one minute more before I try another plan."

Mr. Morton took out his watch, and looked at it; the boys who had not been engaged in the mischief looked virtuously around them, and the guilty boys looked at their desks.

"Now," exclaimed Mr. Morton, replacing his watch in his pocket. "Stand up like men. Will none of you do it?"

Benny Mallow whispered, "Yes, sir," but the teacher did not hear him; besides, Benny made no effort to keep his word, so his whispering amounted to nothing.

"Grayson," said Mr. Morton, "come here."

Bert Sharp, who sat near the front of the room, where the teacher could watch him, edged to the end of his seat, so as to be ready to jump up and run away the moment Grayson told—if he dared to tell. Most of the other boys found their hearts so high in their throats that they could not swallow them again, as Grayson, looking very white and uncomfortable, stepped to the front.

"Grayson," said the teacher, "I have known you for many months: have I ever been unkind to you?"

"No, sir," replied Grayson; then he wiped his eyes; seeing which, Bert Sharp thought he might as well run now as later, for boys who began by crying always ended by telling.

"You saw the attack made on the Italian; Justice Stott says you admitted as much to him. Now I want you to tell me who were of the party."

"May I speak first, sir?" asked Grayson.

"Yes," said the teacher.

"Boys," said Grayson, half facing the school,

"MR. MORTON, I WAS THERE."

"you all hate a tell-tale, and so do I. Do you think it the fair thing to hold your tongues and make a tell-tale of me?"

Grayson looked at Will Palmer as he spoke, but Will only looked sulky in return; then Grayson looked at Benny Mallow, and Benny was fast making up his mind that he would tell rather than have his friend do it, when up stood Bert Sharp and said,

"Mr. Morton, I was there."

"Bravo, Sharp!" exclaimed the teacher. "Grayson, you may take your seat. Sharp, step to the front. Now, boys, who is man enough to stand beside Sharp?"

"I am," piped Benny Mallow, and he almost ran in his eagerness.

"It's no use," whispered Will Palmer to Ned Johnston, and the two boys went to the front together; then there was a general uprising, and a scramble to see who should not be last.

"Good!" exclaimed Mr. Morton, looking at the

culprits and then about the school·room; "I believe you're all here. I'm proud of you, boys. You
did a shameful thing in attacking a harmless man,
but you have done nobly by confessing. I cannot
let you off without punishment, but you will suffer
far less than you would have done by successfully
concealing your fault. None of you are to go out
at recess next week. Now go to your seats. Sharp,
you may take any unoccupied desk you like. After
this I think I can trust you to behave yourself
without being watched."

The boys had never before seen Sharp look as
he did as he walked to a desk in the back of the
room and sat down. As soon as the bell was struck
for recess Grayson hurried over to Sharp and said,

"You helped me out of a terrible scrape, do you
know it?"

"I'm glad of it," said Sharp. "And that isn't
all; I wish I could think of something else to own
up to."

Chapter V.

THOSE JAIL-BIRDS.

LTHOUGH the people of Laketon could not forgive Mr. Morton and Paul Grayson for not talking more about themselves and their past lives, they could not deny that both the teacher and his pupil were of decided value to the town. All the boys, whether in Mr. Morton's school or the public school, seemed to like Paul Grayson when they became acquainted with him, and the parents of the boys sensibly argued that there could not be anything very bad about a boy who was so popular. Besides, the other boys in talking about Paul declared that he never swore and never lied; and as lying and swearing were the two vices most common among the Laketon boys, and therefore most hated by the parents, they felt that there was

5

at least no occasion to regard the new - comer with suspicion.

As for Mr. Morton, he rapidly made his way among the more solid citizens. He was willing to work, whether his services were required by church, Sunday-school, or society, and he did not care to hold office of any sort, so his sincerity was cheerfully admitted by all. When, however, he had one day, soon after his arrival, asked several prominent men why the town had no society, or even person, to visit the very poor and the persons who might be in prison, he ran some risk of being considered meddlesome.

"We know our own people best," said Sam Wardwell's father. "The only people here who suffer from poverty are those who won't work, while the few people who get into our jail are hard cases; half of them wouldn't listen to you if you talked to them, and the others would listen only to have an excuse to beg tobacco or something. There's a man in the jail now for passing counterfeit money; he's committed for trial when the County Court sits in

September; that man is just as smart as you or I. He is as fine a looking fellow as you would wish to see, talks like a straightforward business man, and yet he passed counterfeit bills at four different places in this town. What would talk do for such a fellow?"

"No one knows until some one tries it," replied the teacher, quietly.

"Well, all I have to say is," remarked Mr. Wardwell, in a tone that was intended to be very sarcastic, "those who have plenty of time to waste must do the trying. If you want such work done, why don't you do it yourself?"

"I would cheerfully do it if it did not seem to be presumptuous on the part of a stranger."

"Don't trouble your mind about that," said the store-keeper, with a laugh; "the counterfeiter is a stranger too, so matters will be even. There's the sheriff, in front of the post-office; do you know him? No? Let us step over, and I'll introduce you; and I'll wish you more luck than you'll have in the jail, if that will be of any consolation."

Mr. Morton found Sheriff Towler quite a pleasant man to talk to, and perfectly willing to have his
prisoners improve in body and mind by any method
except that of getting out of jail before their respective terms of imprisonment had expired, or before
they were by superior authority ordered to some
other place of confinement, as he, the sheriff, wished
might at once be the case with John Doe, the man
who was awaiting trial for passing bad bank-notes.
All this the sheriff said as he walked with Mr. Morton from the post-office to the jail. Arrived at the
last-named building, the sheriff instructed his deputy,
who had charge of the place, to admit Mr. Morton
at any time that gentleman might care to converse
with any of the prisoners.

The teacher walked first through the upper rooms,
where a small but choice assortment of habitual
drunkards and petty thieves were confined; these,
as Sam Wardwell's father had predicted, either declined to converse or talked stupidly for a moment
or two, and then begged either tobacco or money to

buy it with. Still, Mr. Morton thought he saw in these wretched fellows some material to work upon, when time allowed. Then he went below, and the deputy took him to the small grated window in the door of the strong cell for desperate offenders, and said to John Doe that a gentleman who was visiting the prisoners would like to·speak with him. The deputy went away immediately after saying this, and Mr. Morton quickly put his face to the grated window. A face appeared on the other side of the grating, and then, as Mr. Morton placed his hand between the bars, which were barely wide enough apart to admit it, he felt his fingers grasped most earnestly by the hand of the prisoner. If Mr. Wardwell could have felt that grasp and seen the prisoner's face, he might have greatly changed his opinion ·of· smart prisoners in general.

Somehow John Doe preferred to restrict his remarks to whispers, and for some reason Mr. Morton humored him. The interview lasted but a few moments, and ended with a plea and a promise that another call should be made. Meanwhile, Mr. Wardwell had stood on a corner that commanded the jail, and when the teacher reappeared the merchant asked, " Well ?"

" They are a sad set," Mr. Morton admitted.

" I told you so," said Wardwell, rubbing his hands, as if he were glad rather than sorry that the prisoners were as bad as he had thought them. " And how did you find that rascally counterfeiter? I'll warrant he didn't care to see you ?"

" On the contrary," replied the teacher, gravely, " he was very glad to see me. He begged me to come again. He was so glad to see some one not a jailer that he cried."

" Well, I never !" exclaimed the merchant. And he told the truth.

It was soon after this first visit of a series that lasted as long as Mr. Morton remained in the village that the boys changed their base-ball ground. They had generally played in some open ground on the edge of the town, but the teacher one day asked why

they should go so far, when the entire square on
which the court-house and jail stood was vacant, except for those two buildings. The boys spent a
whole recess in considering this suggestion; then
they reported it favorably to the other boys of the
town, and it was adopted almost unanimously that
very week; and Canning Forbes could always remember even the day of the month on which the
first game was played, for he, as a "fielder," caught
the ball exactly on the tip of the longest finger of
his left hand, and he stayed home with that finger,
and woke up nights with it, for a full week afterward.

Paul Grayson had not attended Mr. Morton's
school a fortnight before every one knew that ball
was his favorite game. This preference on the part
of the new boy did not entirely please Benny Mallow, who preferred to have his new friend play marbles, and with him alone, because then he could talk
to him a great deal; whereas at ball, even "town-
ball," which needed but four boys to a game, there

was not much opportunity for talking, while at base-
ball the chances were less, even were Benny not so
generally out of breath when he met Grayson on a
" base " that conversation was impossible.

But Grayson clung to ball; he did not seem to
care much for it in the school - yard, which, indeed,
was rather small for such games, but after school
was dismissed in the afternoons he always tried to
get up a game on the new grounds, and he generally
succeeded. Even boys who did not care particularly for the sport had been told by Mr. Morton that
about the only diversion of the wretched men in
the jail was to look out the window while ball-play-
ing was going on; and as Mr. Morton had begun to
attain special popularity through his work among
the prisoners, the boys who liked him, as most of
them did, were glad to help him to the small extent
they were able.

" I really can't see why Grayson should be so fond
of ball," said Canning Forbes one afternoon, as he
and several other boys lay under the big elm - tree

behind the court-house and criticised the boys who were playing. "He isn't much of a pitcher, he doesn't bat very well, and he often loses splendid chances, while he's catcher, by not seeming to see the ball when it's coming. I wonder if his eyes can be bad?"

"I don't believe they are," said Will Palmer; "he is keen-sighted enough about everything else. Absent-mindedness is his great trouble; every once in a while he gets his eyes fixed on something as if he couldn't move them."

"He gets into a brown-study, you mean," suggested Forbes.

"That's it," assented Will.

"He's thinking about the splendors of the royal home that he is being kept away from," said Napoleon Nott. "You just ought to read what sort of a place a royal home is," continued Notty. "I'll bring up a book about it some day, and read it aloud to all of you fellows."

"No you won't, Notty," said Canning Forbes; "not if we have any legs left to run away with."

Some internal hints that supper-time was approach-ing broke up the game, and the boys moved off the ground, by twos and threes, until only Paul and Ben-ny remained. Paul seemed in no particular hurry to start, and as Benny never seemed to imagine that Paul could see himself safely home from any place, he remained too.

"Benny," said Paul, suddenly, "did you ever see any one in jail?"

"No," said Benny, "I never did."

"Neither did I," said Paul, "but I'm curious to do so now. You needn't go with me; the sight might pain you too much."

"What! Just to go to the jail, and look up at the windows? Oh no; *that* won't hurt me. I've done that lots of times."

"Very well," said Paul, moving toward the jail. He looked up at the windows as he walked; finally he stopped where he could look fairly at the small window of the cell where the counterfeiter was. The sun was not shining upon that side of the jail, so

THE WINDOW OF THE COUNTERFEITER'S CELL.

Benny could barely see there was a face behind the window. Evidently the prisoner was standing on a chair, for the little window was quite high. Paul's eyes seemed better than Benny's, however, for he continued looking at that window for some moments. When he finally turned away, it was because he could not see any longer, for his eyes were full of tears.

"Why, you're crying!" exclaimed Benny, in some astonishment. "What is the matter?"

"I'm so sorry for the poor fellow," replied Paul.

"I am too," said Benny—"awfully sorry. I wish I could cry about it, but somehow my eyes don't work right to-day. Some days I can cry real easily. Next time one of those days comes, I'll come over here with you, and let you see what I can do."

CHAPTER VI.

THE BEANTASSEL BENEFIT.

F the many boys who were curious about Paul Grayson's antecedents, no one devoted more attention to the subject than Benny Mallow. Benny was short, and Paul was tall; Benny was fat, and Paul was thin; Benny's hair was light, while Paul's was black as jet; Benny had light blue eyes, while those of Paul were of a rich brown; Benny always had something to say about himself, while Paul never seemed to think his affairs of the slightest interest ·to any one but himself: so, taking all things into account, it is not wonderful that Benny Mallow spent whole half-hours in contemplating his friend with admiration and wonder.

Still more, as Benny had been accepted by every one as Paul's particular friend, he actually was be-

sieged with all sorts of questions, and to answer
these without letting himself down in the estima-
tion of the school was no easy matter, when he did
not know any more about Paul than any one else
did. One question, however, he settled to the entire
satisfaction of every one but Napoleon Nott—Grayson was not an exiled prince. Benny was sure of
this, because he had asked Paul if he had ever been
on the other side of the ocean, and Paul had answered that he had not. Notty endeavored to
make light of this evidence by showing how easy
it would have been to spirit the mysterious person
away from his royal home and to America while he
was a baby, and therefore too young to know anything about it; but Will Palmer told Notty that it
was about time to stop making a fool of himself,
and the other boys present said they thought so too,
at which Notty became so angry that he vowed, in
the presence of at least a dozen boys, that when
the truth came out, and all the boys wanted to bor-
row his copy of "The Exiled Prince: a Tale of

Woe," he would not lend it to them, even if it were to save them from death; he would not even let them look at the cover, with its picture of the prince and the name of the publisher.

Meanwhile Mr. Morton had continued his visits to the prisoners and to the poor of the town, and out of school hours he had so interested the boys in some of the suffering families of worthless men or widowed women, that it was agreed by the whole school that the teasing of any of the boys of these families about the holes in their trousers, or provoking fights with or between them, should entirely stop; indeed, as this suggestion came from Bert Sharp, who was fonder of fighting than any other boy in the town, the school could not well do other' wise.

The boys went even farther: when one day old Peter Beantassel, whose family was always on the verge of starvation, spent on drink the accidental earnings of a week, and then fell into an abandoned well and was drowned, it was decided by the school

to give an exhibition for the benefit of Mrs. Beantassel and her six children. Mr. Morton was delighted, and promised to secure a church or hall
without expense to the boys, and to collect enough
money from the public to pay for printing the tickets. The boys at once began work in tremendous
earnest; they were for a fortnight so busy at determining upon a programme, and studying, rehears-
ing, selling tickets, and exacting promises from people who would not purchase in advance, that there
was but little playing before school and during
recess, blackberry hedges were neglected, and the
trout in the single brook near the town had not the
slightest excuse for apprehension.

Paul Grayson entered into the spirit of the occasion as thoroughly as any one else; he volunteered to recite Longfellow's "Psalm of Life," and
when the farce of "Box and Cox" was about to be
given up because no boy was willing to dress up
in women's clothes, and be laughed at by all the
larger girls, for playing the part of Mrs. Bouncer,

Paul volunteered for that unpopular character, and saved the play. But this was not all. There were to be some tableaux; and as Mr. Morton had been asked to suggest some scenes, particularly one or two with Indians in them, and was as fond of pointing a moral as teachers usually are, one of his tableaux, to be called "Civilization," was a scene in the interior of an Indian's wigwam. The squaw, who had just been killed, was lying dead on the floor; her husband, with his hands tied, stood bleeding between two soldiers, while between father and mother stood the half-grown son, wondering what it all was about. As all of the boys wanted to see this tragic picture, all of them declined to take part in it; Joe Appleby had been heard to remark with a sneer that only very small and green boys cared to look at Indians, so he was asked to take the part of the wretched son himself; but he said that when any one saw him making a fool of himself by browning his face and dressing up in rags, he hoped some one would tell him about it: so

Grayson, as the only other tall boy who had dark hair that was not cut short, was cast for this part also, and offered no objection. As for the bleeding chieftain, Napoleon Nott fought hard to pose in that character, and was quieted only by being allowed to play the dead squaw, which all the boys told him he ought easily to see was the more romantic part, besides being one in which he could by no chance make any mistake.

The place selected for the entertainment was the lecture-room of the Presbyterian church, and the boys had therefore to give up their darling project of devoting half an hour of the evening to amateur negro minstrelsy; for one of the deacons said that while he sometimes doubted that even an organ was a proper musical instrument for use in sacred buildings, he certainly was not going to tolerate banjos and bones. This decision was a great disappointment to Benny Mallow, who had been selected by the managers to perform upon the tambourine, but in the revision of the programme Benny was assigned to duty in a tableau as a little fat goblin, and this so tickled his fancy that he did not suffer long by the disappointment.

At last the eventful night arrived. Some of the boys did not leave the lecture-room at all after the last rehearsal, not even to get their suppers, for fear they should be late, and those who reached the room barely in time to take their parts had all they could do to squeeze through the crowd that blocked the doors and filled the aisles. The spectacle of so crowded a house raised the boys to a high pitch of excitement, which was increased by various peeps, from the curtains that served as dressing-rooms, at the Beantassel children, who by some thoughtful soul had been provided with free seats in the extreme front bench; there they were, all but the baby; they had been provided with clothing which, though old, was far more sightly than the rags they usually wore, and although they did not seem as much at ease as some others among the spectators, their eyes stood so very open, then and throughout

the evening, that even Joe Appleby, who had re-
luctantly consented to pose, in his best clothes, with
gloves, cane, and high hat, as Young America in a
tableau of "The Nations," agreed with himself
that the exhibition was rather a meritorious idea
after all, and that even if the boys did as badly
as he knew they would, he was glad it was sure
to pay.

But the boys did not do badly; on the contrary,
the general performance would have been quite
creditable to adults. The opening was somewhat
dismal; it was announced to consist of a duet for
two flutes by Will Palmer and Ned Johnston. The
boys had practised industriously at several airs in
order to discover which would be best, and at last
they supposed they had fully agreed; but when
seated Ned began the *Miserere* from "Trovatore,"
while Will started "The Old Folks at Home;" and
each was sure the other was wrong, and would cor-
rect himself, which the other in both cases failed to
do; the two boys finally retired abruptly, amid con-

siderable laughter, and fought the matter out in the
dressing-room. ⨉

Paul Grayson soon restored order, however, by
his rendering of the "Psalm of Life." He had a
fine voice, and he spoke the lines as if he meant
them; so gloriously did his voice ring that even
the boys in the dressing-room kept silence and listened, though they had heard the same verses a
hundred times before.

Most of the performances that followed went
very smoothly, although Benny Mallow, who played
the Hatter's part in "Box and Cox," caused some
confusion by laughing frequently and unexpectedly,
because Paul's disguise as Mrs. Bouncer affected
him powerfully in spite of the efforts made by Sam
Wardwell, as the Printer, to restrain him. The tableaux pleased the audience greatly; even that of
"Prometheus," with Ned Johnston as the sufferer,
and Mrs. Battle's big red rooster as the vulture,
brought down the house.

But the great tableau of the evening was the

teacher's " Civilization." When Paul Grayson had understood fully what the scene was to be, he re- fused so earnestly to have anything to do with it that the boys were startled. They did not excuse him from taking the part of the young Indian, however; they pleaded so steadily that at last Paul consented, but in worse temper than any one had ever seen him before. No one could complain of the manner in which he acted on the stage, how- ever. When the curtain was drawn he was seen standing beside his dead mother, and shaking a fist at the soldiers; in color, dress, pose, and spirit he seemed to be a real Indian, if the audience was a competent judge; then, when the applause justified a recall, as it soon did, the drawn curtain disclosed Paul clinging to the wounded brave as if nothing should ever tear him away.

Napoleon Nott saw all this, although, as the Indian boy's mother, he was supposed to be dead beyond recall. Suddenly he felt himself to be inspired, and when the curtain was down he flew into the dressing-room and exclaimed, "I've got it!"

"Be careful not to hurt it," said Canning Forbes, sarcastically.

"I've got it!" declared Notty, without noticing Canning's cruel speech. "Grayson is an Indian, a chief's son. You don't suppose he could have made believe so well as all that, do you? That's it. I knew he was a great person of some sort. Sh—h! he's coming."

Somehow the boys who had been able to peep out at the tableau did not laugh at Notty this time. Paul, in his Indian dress, had greatly impressed them all before he left the dressing-room, and certainly his acting had been unlike anything the boys had seen other boys do. The subject was talked over in whispers, so that Paul should not hear, during the remainder of the evening, with the result that that very night at least six boys told other boys or their own parents, in the strictest confidence, of course, that there was more truth than make-believe about Paul Grayson as an Indian. And the parents told the same story to other parents, the boys told it to other boys, and within twenty-four hours Paul Grayson was a far more interesting mystery than before.

CHAPTER VII.

A BEAUTIFUL THEORY RUINED.

WHEN Benny Mallow went to bed at night, after the great exhibition, he suddenly re- membered that he had forgotten to ask what the grand total of the receipts for the Bean- tassel family had been. Under ordinary circum- stances he would have got out of bed, dressed him- self, and scoured the town for full information be- fore he slept. On this particular night, however, he did not give the subject more than a moment of thought, for his mind was full of greater things. Paul Grayson an Indian? Why, of course: how had he been so stupid as not to think of it before? Paul was only dark, while Indians were red, but then it was easy enough for him to have been a half-breed; Paul was very straight, as Indians always were in books; Paul was a splendid shot with a rifle, as all Indians are; Paul had no parents— well, the tableau made by Paul's own friend, Mr. Morton, who knew all about him, explained plainly enough how Indian boys came to be without fathers and mothers.

Even going to sleep did not rid Benny of these thoughts. He saw Paul in all sorts of places all through the night, and always as an Indian. At one time he was on a wild horse, galloping madly at a wilder buffalo; then he was practising with bow and arrow at a genuine archery target; then he stood in the opening of a tent made of skins; then he lay in the tall grass, rifle in hand, awaiting some deer that were slowly moving toward him. He even saw Paul tomahawk and scalp a white boy of his own size, and although the face of the victim was that of Joe Appleby, the hair somehow was long enough to tie around the belt which Paul, like all Indians in picture-books, wore for the express purpose of providing properly for the scalps he took.

So fully did Benny's dreams take possession of him, that, although he had been awake for two hours the next morning before he met Paul, he was rather startled and considerably disappointed to find his friend in ordinary dress, without a sign of belt, scalp, or tomahawk about him. Still, of course Paul was an Indian, and Benny promptly determined that no one should beat him in getting information about the young man's earlier life; so Benny opened conversation abruptly by asking, "Where do you begin to cut when you want to take a man's scalp off?"

"Why, who are you going to scalp, little fellow?" asked Paul.

"Oh, nobody," said Benny, in confusion. "I'd like to know, that's all."

"I'm afraid you'll have to ask some one else, then," said Paul, with a laugh. "Try me on something easier."

"Then how do you ride a wild horse without saddle or bridle?" asked Benny.

"Worse and worse," said Paul. "See here, Benny, have you been reading dime novels, and made up your mind to go West?"

"Not exactly," said Benny; "but," he continued, "I wouldn't mind going West if I had some good safe fellow to go with—some one who has been there and knows all about it."

"Well, I know enough about it to tell you to stay at home," said Paul.

This was proof enough, thought Benny; so, although he was aching to ask Paul many other questions about Indian life, he hurried off to assure the other boys that it was all right—that Paul was an Indian, and no mistake. The consequence was that when Paul approached the school-house half of the boys advanced slowly to meet him, and then they clustered about him, and he became conscious of being looked at even more intently than on the day of his first appearance. He did not seem at all pleased by the attention; he looked rather angry, and then turned pale; finally he hurried up-stairs into the school-room and whispered something to the teacher, at which Mr. Morton shook his head and patted Paul on the shoulder, after which the boy regained his ease and took his seat.

But at recess he again found himself the centre of a crowd, no member of which seemed to care to begin any sort of game. Paul stopped short, looked around him, frowned, and asked, "Boys, what is the matter with me?"

"Nothing," replied Will Palmer.

"Then what are you all crowding around me for?"

No one answered for a moment, but finally Sam Wardwell said, "We want you to tell us stories."

"Stories about Indians," explained Ned Johnston.

Paul laughed. "You're welcome to all I know," said he; "but I don't think they're very interesting. Really, I can't remember a single one that's worth telling."

This was very discouraging; but Canning Forbes, who was so smart that, although he was only four-teen years of age, he was studying mental philosophy, whispered to Will Palmer that people never saw anything interesting about their own daily lives.

"You can tell us something about birch canoes, can't you?" asked Ned Johnston, by way of encour-agement.

"Oh yes," Paul replied; "they're made out of bark, with hoops and strips of wood inside, to give them shape and make them strong."

"How do they fasten up the ends?" asked Ned.

"They first sew or tie them together with strings, and then they put pitch over the seams to make them water-tight."

"Did you ever see the Indians race in birch canoes?" asked Sam.

"Oh yes, often," Paul replied; "and they make fast time too, I can tell you."

"Did you ever race yourself?" asked Benny.

"No," said Paul, "but I learned to paddle a ca-noe pretty well. I'd rather have a good row-boat, though, than any birch I ever saw. If you run one of them on a sharp stone, it may be cut open, unless it's pretty new."   .

" How do the Indians kill buffaloes?" asked Will Palmer.

" Why, just as white men do—they shoot them with rifles. Nearly all the Indians have rifles now-adays."

This was very unromantic, most of the boys thought, for an Indian without bows and arrows could not be very different from a white man. Still, something wonderful would undoubtedly come before Paul was done talking.

"Are buffaloes really so terrible-looking as the story-papers say?" asked Bert Sharp.

" Well, they don't look exactly like pets," said Paul. "A bull buffalo, in the winter season, when he has a full coat of hair, looks fiercer than a lion."

" Do the Indians really kill or torture all the white people they catch?" asked Canning Forbes.

" I don't know—I suppose so; but perhaps they're not all as bad as some white people say."

"YOU'RE A CHIEF'S SON, AREN'T YOU?"

Canning shook his head encouragingly at Will Palmer: evidently this young Indian had a manly spirit, and was not going to have his people abused. There was a moment or two of silence, each boy wondering what next to ask. Finally, Napoleon Nott said,

" You're a chief's son, aren't you ?"

" What?" exclaimed Paul, so sharply that Notty dodged behind Will Palmer, and put his hand to his head as if to protect his scalp.

" I meant," said Notty, tremblingly—" I meant to ask what tribe you belonged to."

" I ? What tribe? Notty, what are you talking about ?"

Notty did not answer; so Paul looked around at the other boys, but they also were silent.

" Notty," said Paul, " what on earth are you thinking about? Do you imagine I'm an Indian ?"

" I thought you were," said Notty, very meekly; " and," he continued, " so did all the other boys."

"Well, that's good," said Paul, laughing heartily. "What made you think so, fellows?"

"Benny told us," explained Ned.

"Benny?" exclaimed Paul. "What put that fancy into your head?"

"I—I dreamed it," said Benny, almost ready to cry for shame and disappointment.

"And you told all the other boys?"

"Yes, I believed it; I really did, or I never would have said it."

Then Paul laughed again—a long, hearty laugh it was, but no one helped him. Most of the boys felt as if in some way Paul had cheated them. As for Ned Johnston, he evidently did not believe Paul, for he began to ask questions.

"If you're not an Indian, how do you know so much about a birch canoe?"

"Why, I've seen dozens of them in Maine, where I used to live; the Indians make them there."

"Wild Indians?" asked Ned, and all the boys listened eagerly for the answer.

"No," said Paul, contemptuously; "they're the tamest kind of tame ones."

This was dreadful, yet Ned thought he would try once more. "How did you come to know so much about buffaloes?" he asked.

"I saw two in Central Park, in New York," Paul replied. "Oh, boys! boys! you're dreadfully sold."

"Say, Paul," said Benny, edging to the front, and looking appealingly at his friend, "you've been away out West, anyhow, haven't you?—because you told me you knew about it." Benny awaited the answer with fear and trembling, for he felt he never would hear the end of the affair if he did not get some help from Paul.

"No, I've never been farther West than Laketon," was the disheartening reply. "All I know of the West I've learned from books and newspapers."

"Dear me!" sighed Benny; and for the first time in his life he wished the bell would ring, and give him an excuse to get away. Within a moment his wish was gratified, and he scampered up-stairs very briskly, but not before Bert Sharp had caught up with him, and called him "Smarty," and asked him if he hadn't some more dreams that he could go about telling as truth. Poor Benny's only consola-tion, as he took his seat, was that Notty had been the first to suggest the Indian theory, and he ought therefore to bear a part of whatever abuse might come of the mistake.

At any rate, he had learned that Paul had been in Maine and New York; certainly that was more than he had known an hour before.

Chapter VIII.

DARED.

OR a day or two after the terrible collapse of the Indian theory Paul Grayson kept himself aloof from the other boys to such an extent that he made them feel very uncomfortable. Benny, in particular, was made most miserable by such treatment from Paul, for Benny was not happy unless he could talk a great deal; and as he could not even be near the other boys without being reproached for his untruthful Indian story, the coolness of Paul reduced him to the necessity of doing all his talking at home, where he really could not spend time enough to tell all that was on his mind.

Besides, there were several darling topics on which Benny's mother and sister, although they loved the boy dearly, never would exhibit any interest. Benny had lately learned, after months of wearisome practice in Sam Wardwell's barn, that peculiar gymnastic somersault known and highly esteemed among boys of a certain age as "skinning the cat," and he was dying to have some one see him do it, and praise him for his skill. But when he proposed to do it in the house, from the top of one of the door frames, his mother called him inhuman, and his sister said he was disgusting, the instant they heard the name of the trick; and although Benny finally made them understand that cats had really nothing to do with the trick, and that if he should ever want the skin taken off a real cat he would not do the work himself, not even for the best fishing-rod in town, he was still as far from succeeding as ever; for when he afterward explained just what the trick consisted in, his mother told him that he was her only boy, and while she liked to see him amuse himself, she never would consent to stand still and look at him while he was attempting to break his blessed little neck.

And how unsatisfactory his sister was when consulted about fish bait! In marbles she had been known to exhibit some interest, but a boy could not always talk about marbles. When Benny explained how different kinds of live bait kicked while on the hook, and asked her to think of some new kind of bug or insect that he could try on the big trout that had learned to escape trouble by letting alone the insects already used to hide hooks with, she told him that she didn't know anything about it, and, what was more, she didn't care to, and she didn't think her brother was a very nice boy to care for such dirty things himself.

The change in the relations of the boys with Paul did not escape Mr. Morton's eyes; and when he questioned his newest pupil, and learned the cause, he made an excuse to send Paul home for something, and then told the boys that to pry into the affairs of other people was most unmannerly, and that he thought Paul had been too good a fellow to deserve such treatment at the hands of his companions. The boys admitted to themselves that they thought so

too; and when next they were out-of-doors together
most of them agreed with each other that there
should be no more questioning of Paul Grayson
about himself. Still, Sam Wardwell correctly expressed the sentiment of the entire school when he
said he hoped that Paul would soon think to tell
without being asked, because it was certain that
there was something wonderful about him; boys
were not usually as cool, strong, good-natured, fear-
less, and sensible as he.

Pleasant relations were soon restored between the
boys, but there was not as much playing in the
school-yard as before, for the weather had become
very hot; so the usual diversion of the boys was to
sit in a row on the lower rail of the shady side of
the school-yard fence, and tell stories, or agree upon
what to do when the evening became cooler. Paul
Grayson occasionally begged for a game of ball; he
could not bear to be so lazy, he said, even if the sun
did shine hotly. But the boys could seldom agree
with him to the extent of playing on the shadeless

ball-ground; so after dismissal in the afternoon Paul used to go alone to the ball-ground behind the court-house, and practise running, hopping, jumping, and tossing a heavy stone, until some of the boys, not having promised to abstain from talking with each other about Paul, wondered if their mysterious friend might not be the son of some great clown, or circus rider, or trapeze performer, or something of the sort. Paul's exercises seemed to give a great deal of en-tertainment to the prisoners in the jail, for some of them were always at the large barred window, and the counterfeiter was sure to be at the small one the moment he heard Paul come whistling by; and well he might, for that cell, lighted only by a single very small window, must have been a dismal place to spend whole days in.

From occasionally looking at the prisoners from the play-ground Paul finally came to stare at them for several minutes at a time. The other boys could not see what there could be about such a lot of bad men to interest a fine fellow like Paul; but Canning

Forbes explained that perhaps the spectacle would
be interesting to them too if they were strangers,
and had not seen the prisoners in every - day life,
and known what a common, stupid, uninteresting
set they were. All of the boys, Canning reminded
them, had been full of curiosity about the counterfeiter when he had first been put into the jail; that,
he explained, was because the man was a stranger,
and no one of them knew a thing about him. Paul
was in exactly the same condition about the other
prisoners, and the counterfeiter too.

The explanation was satisfactory, but Paul's interest in the prisoners was not, for all the time he
spent staring at the side of the jail might otherwise
have been spent with them, all of whom, excepting
perhaps Joe Appleby, felt that they never could see
enough of Paul. Some of them were shrewd enough
to reason that if Paul could be made to understand
what a miserable set those jail-birds really were, he
would soon cease to have any interest in them; so
they made various excuses to talk about the prison-

ers by name, and tell what mean and dishonest and disgraceful things they did.

But somehow the scheme did not work; Paul himself talked about the prisoners, and he remind-ed the boys that some of those men had wives who were being unhappy about them; and others, par-ticularly the younger ones, were keeping loving mothers in misery; and perhaps some of them had children that were suffering, even starving, be-cause their fathers were in jail. How could any fellow help being curious about men, asked Paul, whose condition put such stories into a man's mind?

"Perhaps, too," Paul argued, "some of those men are not as bad as they seem. Every man has a lit-tle good of some sort in him; and although he is to blame for not letting it, instead of his wrong thoughts, manage him, perhaps some day he may change. I can't help wishing so about all of those fellows in the jail, and, what is more, I wouldn't help it if I could—would you?"

No, they wouldn't, the boys thought; still, they thought also, although no one felt exactly like saying it aloud, that boys at Mr. Morton's school had some good in them, and were a great deal surer to appreciate the thoughtful tendencies of a good fellow than a lot of worthless town loafers were, to say nothing of a dreadful counterfeiter.

"If you feel that way," said Joe Appleby, somewhat sneeringly, after the crowd had been silent for two or three moments, "why don't you go with Mr. Morton when he visits the prisoners? I would do it if I felt as you do; I would think it very wrong to stay away."

Joe's tone, as he said this, was so absolutely taunting that most of the boys expected to see Paul spring at him and strike him; they certainly would do so themselves, if big enough, and talked to in that way. But Paul merely replied, "I don't go, because he never asked me to."

"Oh, don't let that stand in your way," said Joe, quickly; "you can easily do the asking yourself.

I'll ask for you, if you feel delicate about putting in your own word."

At this the boys felt sure there would be a fight, but to their great surprise Paul sat quietly on the rail, and replied, "I should be much obliged if you would; that is, if you're man enough to own that you first taunted me about it."

Joe arose, and looked as proud as if he were about to lead a whole army to certain victory.

"I'll do it," said he, " and right away, too."

" And I," said Canning Forbes, " will go along to see that you tell the story correctly, and do full justice to Grayson."

Joe scowled terribly at this, but Canning, although a very quiet fellow, had such a determined way in everything he undertook, that Joe knew it was useless to remonstrate, so he strode sullenly along, with Canning at his side. The other boys looked for a moment in utter astonishment; then, as with one accord, all but Paul sprung to their feet and followed.

Mr. Morton was astonished at the irruption, as

his bell had not been sounded; but he listened to
Joe's request and to Canning's statement, which was
supported by fragments volunteered by other boys;
then he replied, " I will gladly take Paul with me,
but am sorry that the newest pupil in the school
should be the first to express a kind thought about
the unfortunates in the jail."

Then Joe Appleby hung his head, and Canning
Forbes did likewise, and most of the other boys followed their example; but Benny rushed to the side
window, thrust his head out, and shouted, " It's all
right, Paul; he says you can go."

Then all the boys laughed at Benny, at which
Benny blushed, and the teacher rung his bell, which
called in no one but Paul. Then the school came to
order; but most of the boys blundered over their
lessons that afternoon, for their minds were full of
what they had to tell to boys that attended other
schools, or did not go to school at all.

The visit of Paul to the prison was made that
very afternoon, and before night nearly every family

in the town had heard of how it had come to pass, and determined that Paul Grayson was a noble fellow, no matter how much mystery there might be about him. Benny Mallow, having learned in advance that the visit was contemplated — for Paul could not get rid of him after school except by telling him — Benny waited at a corner near the jail until Paul and the teacher came out. He hid himself for a moment or two, so that Paul would not think he had been watching him; then he hurried around a block, intercepted the couple, and made some excuse to stop Paul for a moment. As soon as Mr. Morton had gone ahead a little way, Benny, with his great blue eyes wider open than ever, asked, "How was it?"

"It was dreadful," said Paul, whose eyes were red, as if he had been crying.

"Then you won't ever go again, will you?" said Benny, giving his friend's hand a sympathetic squeeze.

"Yes, I will," exclaimed Paul, so sharply that

8

Benny was frightened. He looked up inquiringly, and saw Paul's eyes filled with tears. " I'll go again, and often, now that I've been teased into doing it; but, Benny Mallow, if you tell a single boy that I cried, I'll never speak to you again in this world."

"I won't—oh, I won't," said Benny, and he kept his word—for weeks.

PAUL GRAYSON AND BENNY MALLOW.

Chapter IX.

BENNY'S PARTY.

R. MORTON'S school closed on the last day of June, and the parents of the pupils were so well pleased with the progress their sons had made that almost all of them thanked the teacher, besides paying him, and they hoped that he would open it again in the autumn. Mr. Morton thanked the gentlemen in return, and said he would think about it; he was not certain that he could afford to begin a new term unless more pupils were promised, although he did not believe the entire county could supply better boys than those he had already taught at Laketon.

The boys, when they heard this, determined that they would not be outdone in the way of compliment, so they resolved, at a full meeting held in

Sam Wardwell's father's barn, that Mr. Morton was a brick, and the class would prove it by giving him as handsome a gold watch-chain as could be bought by a contribution of fifty cents from each of the twenty - three boys. Every boy paid in his fifty cents, although some of them had to part with spe-cial treasures in order to get the money. Benny Mallow sacrificed his whole collection of birds' eggs, which included forty - seven varieties, after having first vainly endeavored to raise the money upon two mole-skins, his swimming tights, and a very large lion that he had spent nearly a day in cutting from a menagerie poster. The chain, suitably inscribed, was formally presented in a neat speech by Joe Appleby; Paul Grayson absolutely refused to do it, insisting that Joe was the real head of the school; indeed, Paul himself asked Joe to make the speech, and from that time forth Joe himself pronounced Paul a royal good fellow, and even introduced him to all girls of his acquaintance who wore long dresses.

For at least a month after school closed the boys were as busy at one sort of play and another as if they had a great deal of lost time to make up. Getting ready for the Fourth of July consumed nearly a week, and getting over the accidents of the day took a week more. Some of the boys went fishing every day; others tried boating; two or three made long pedestrian tours—or started on them—and a few went with Mr. Morton and Paul on short mineralogical and botanical excursions.

Then, just as mere sport began to be wearisome, August came in, and the larger fruits of all sorts began to ripen. Fruit was so plenty in and about Laketon that no one attached special value to it; a respectable boy needed only to ask in order to get all he could eat, so boys were invited to each other's gardens to try early apples or plums or pears, and as no boy was exactly sure which particular fruit or variety he most liked, the visits were about as numerous as the varieties. Later in the month the peaches ripened; and as the boy who

could not eat a hatful at a sitting was not considered very much of a fellow, several hours of every
clear day were consumed by attention to peach-trees.

Besides all these delightful duties, a great deal
of talking had to be done about the coming cold
season. Boys who had spent unsatisfactory au-
tumns and winters in other years began in time
to trade for such skates, or sleds, or game bags, or
other necessities as they might be without, and the
result was that some other boys who traded found
themselves in a very bad way when cold weather
came. Between all the occupations named, time
flew so fast that September and the beginning of
another school term were very near at hand before
any boy had half finished all that he had meant to
do during vacation.

There were still some pleasant things to look
forward to, though: court would sit in the first
week of September, and then the counterfeiter
would be tried, while on the very first day of September would come Benny Mallow's birthday party

—an affair that every year was looked forward to with pleasure; for Benny's mother, although far from rich, was very proud of her children, and always made their little companies as pleasant as any ever given in Laketon for young people. When Benny's birthday anniversary arrived, every respectable boy who knew him was sure to be invited, even if he had shamefully cheated Benny in a trade a week before, and Benny generally was cheated when he traded at all, for whatever thing he wanted seemed so immense beside what he had to offer for it, that year by year he seemed to own less and less.

At last the night of the party came, and even Joe Appleby, whose own birthday parties were quite choice affairs, was manly enough to declare that it was the finest thing of the year. The house was tastefully dressed with flowers, which always grew to perfection in Mrs. Mallow's garden, and the lady of the house knew just how to use them to the best advantage. Benny and his sister received the guests; and although Benny was barely twelve years old that day, and rather small for his age, he appeared quite graceful and manly in his new Sunday suit, which had not, like the new suits of most of the Laketon boys, been cut with a view to his growing within the year. His sister Bessie was only a month or two beyond her tenth birthday, but in white muslin and blue ribbons, with her flaxen hair in a long heavy braid on her back, and her bright blue eyes and delicate pink cheeks, she was pretty enough to distract attention from some girls who wore longer dresses, and, indeed, from several girls in very long dresses, who had been invited out of respect for the tastes of Joe Appleby, Will Palmer, and Paul Grayson.

Mrs. Mallow was as successful at entertaining young people as she was in dressing her children and ornamenting her little cottage. She had prepared charades, and given Bessie a lot of new riddles to propose, and she herself played on her rather old piano some airs that the boys enjoyed far more than they did the "exercises" that their sisters were continually drumming. Several of the boys were rather disappointed at there being no kissing games, but they compromised on "choosing partners;" and as there were some guessing tricks, in which the boys who missed had each to select a girl, and retire to the hall with her until a new "guess" was agreed upon, it is quite probable that most of the boys enjoyed opportunities for kissing their particular lady friends at least once or twice.

As for the supper, a month passed before Sam Wardwell could think of it without his mouth watering. There were chicken salad and three kinds of cake, and ice-cream and water ices and lemonade, and oranges and bananas that had come all the way from New York in a box by themselves, and there were mottoes and mixed candies and figs and raisins and English walnuts, while so many of the almonds had double kernels that every girl in the room ate at least two philopenas, and therefore had enough to busy her mind for a day in determining what presents she would claim.

But, in spite of a well-supplied table and forty or fifty appetites that never had been known to fail, full justice was not done to that supper, for while at least half of the company had not got through with the cream and ices, and Sam Wardwell had only had time to taste one kind of cake (having helped himself three times to chicken salad), a small colored boy, who knew by experience that news-carrying levels all ranks, if only the news is great enough, knocked at the door, and asked for Benny. While the door stood ajar, and Mrs. Mallow went in search of her boy, the spectacle of a number of other boys standing in the hall was too much for the colored boy, so he gasped, "De counterfeiter done broke out ob de jail!"

Then there was a time. Two or three of the boys abandoned their partners at once, and hurried to the door to ask questions, while one or two more seized their hats, sneaked toward the back door, walked leisurely out, as if they merely wished to cool off, and then started on a rapid run for the jail.

"DE COUNTERFEITER DONE BROKE OUT OB DE JAIL."

Benny wished to follow them—and not for the purpose of bringing them back, either—and all of his
mother's reasoning powers and authority had to be
exerted to keep her son from forsaking his guests.
Strangest of all, Paul Grayson, who had throughout the evening made himself so agreeable to at
least half a dozen of the young ladies that he was
pronounced just too splendid for anything, had been
among the first to run away! Benny said he never
would have thought it of Paul, and his mother said
the very same thing, while the girls, who but a few
moments before had been loud in his praise, now
clustered together, with very red cheeks, and agreed
that if a mean old counterfeiter was more interesting than a lot of young ladies, why, they were sure
that *Mister* Paul Grayson was entirely welcome to
all he could see of the horrid wretch.

Still, the party went on, after a fashion, although
some of the girls were rather absent-minded for a
few moments, until they had determined what par-
ticularly cutting speeches they would make to their

beaux when next they met them. They did not
have long to wait, for soon the boys came straggling
back, Sam Wardwell being the first to arrive, for,
as on reaching the jail Sam could learn nothing,
and found nothing to look at but the open door
of the empty cell, he shrewdly determined that there
might yet be time to get some more ice-cream if he
hurried back. Somehow none of the girls abused
him; on the contrary, they seemed so anxious to
know all about the escape that Sam was almost
sorry that he had not remained away longer and
learned more.

Then Ned Johnston returned. He had been
lucky enough to meet a man who had wanted to
be deputy-sheriff and jail-keeper, but had failed;
he told Ned that the jailer had stupidly forgotten
to bolt the great door, after having examined the
inside of the cell, as he did every night before re-
tiring, to see if the prisoner had been attempting
to cut through the walls. The prisoner had been
smart enough to listen, and to notice that the bolts

were not shot nor the key turned, so he had quietly walked out; and had not Mr. Wardwell met him on the street, and recognized him in spite of the dark-ness, and hurried off to tell the sheriff, no one would have known of the escape until morning. There was not the slightest chance of catching the pris-oner again, the would-be deputy had said to Ned; there wasn't brains enough in the sheriff and all his staff to get the better of a smart man; but things would be very different if proper men were in office.

When the party finally broke up, several boys were still missing; but as their absence gave sev-eral other boys the chance to escort two girls home instead of one, these faithful beaux determined that they had not lost so very much by remaining, after all.

9

CHAPTER X.

RECAPTURED.

N the morning after Benny Mallow's party hardly a boy started for the brook or the woods. This was not because the dissipation of the previous night had made them over-weary, or too heavy and late a supper had induced headaches, or the party itself had to be talked over. Each of these reasons might have kept a boy or two at home, but the real cause that prevented the majority going about their usual diversions was fear of meeting the escaped counterfeiter. Where the information came from no one thought to inquire; but the report was circulated among the boys quite early in the morning that the criminal was armed with two heavy revolvers that some secret confederate had passed through the window to him, and that he would on no account allow himself to be captured alive.

This story justified the stoutest-hearted boy, even if he owned a rifle, in preferring to keep away from any and all places in which such a person might hide; but the story seemed afterward to have been only half told, for as it passed through Napoleon Nott's lips a bowie-knife, a sword-cane, a bottle of poison, and a long piece of a prison chain were neatly added to the bad man's armament; so no boy felt ashamed to confess to any other boy that he really was afraid to venture beyond the edge of the town.

"You can never tell where such fellows may hide," said Sam Wardwell to several boys who had gathered at the school wood-pile, which was a general rendezvous for boys who had nothing in particular to do. "I've read in the police reports in the New York paper that father takes of policemen finding thieves and murderers and other bad men in the queerest kind of places. They're very fond of hiding in stables."

"Then I know one thing," said Ned Johnston, promptly—"our hens may steal nests all over the hay-loft, and hatch all the late chickens they want to, to die as soon as the frost comes, but I won't go inside of our barn again until that man is found."

"And I'll stay out of our stable," said Bert Sharp, "though it is fun to go in there sometimes, when a fellow hasn't anything else to do, and tickle the horse's flanks to see him kick."

"You ought to be kicked yourself for doing such a mean trick," said Charlie Gunter. "Where else do they hide, Sam?"

"Oh, all sorts of places," said Sam—"sometimes inside of barrels. And just think of it! there's at least twenty empty barrels in the yard of our store, besides a great big hogshead that would hold six counterfeiters."

"Perhaps he's in that hogshead now, with his confederate," suggested Charlie Gunter. "Can't we all get on the roof of the store and look down into it?"

"I won't go," said Ned Johnston, very decidedly; "they might shoot up at us."

"One fellow," continued Sam, "was found buried just under the top of the ground; he just had his nose and mouth out so he could breathe, but he had even those covered with some grass so as to hide them."

"How did he bury himself?" asked Canning Forbes.

"The paper didn't say," answered Sam. "I suppose his pals dug the hole and covered him up."

"My!" exclaimed Benny Mallow. "I won't dare to go out into the garden to gather tomatoes or pull corn for mother."

"Perhaps he's behind that very fence," suggested Napoleon Nott. "I had a book that told about a Frenchman that laid so close against a fence that the police walked right past him without seeing him, and then he got up and killed them, and buried them, and—"

"Keep the rest for to-morrow, Notty," suggested

Canning Forbes; "but put plenty of salt on, so it won't spoil. We've got as much of it as we can swallow to-day."

"I wonder why Paul don't come out?" said Will Palmer.

"He isn't at home," said Benny; "and Mr. Morton is very much worried about him, too; but I told him that he needn't be afraid; that Paul could take care of himself even in a fight with a counterfeiter."

"Good for you, Benny!" exclaimed Will Palmer. "If Paul only had his rifle with him, I'd back him against the worst character in the world. But say, boys, while we're lounging about here the fellow may have been captured and brought back to jail. Let's go up and see."

All that could be learned, when the jail was reached, was that the sheriff had sworn in ten special deputies, and these, with the sheriff himself, were scouring the town and the adjacent country. The sheriff had wanted to make a deputy of Mr. Morton, for men who were sure they could recognize the prisoner at sight were very scarce; but the teacher had excused himself by saying he was not yet legally a citizen of Laketon. Mr. Wardwell said to two or three gentlemen that this was undoubtedly a mere trick to cover the teacher's foolish tenderness toward the prisoner whom he had visited so often, and some of the gentlemen said that they shouldn't wonder if Mr. Wardwell was right.

When dinner-time came, an unforeseen trouble occurred to the boys: they could not go in a crowd to dinner unless some boy felt like inviting the crowd to take dinner with him, and no boy felt justified in doing that unless he first asked his mother whether she had enough for so many; so the party divided, each boy retaining his trusty stick, and going with beating heart past every fence and wood-pile behind which he could not see.

Benny Mallow had just reached home, with his heart away up in the top of his throat, and stuck there so tight that he was sure he could not swallow a mouthful, no matter how nice the dinner might be,

when he saw, crossing his street, and at least a quarter of a mile away, three people, one of whom he was
sure must be Paul. He shaded his eyes, looked intently for an instant, and then became so certain that
it was Paul, whom he felt himself simply dying to
see, that he forgot his heart and his dinner, and even
the danger that might lurk in any one of a dozen
places by the way; he even dropped his stick as
he sped away as fast as he could run. By the time
he reached the place at which he had seen the men
the party was two squares farther to the left, and
Benny was panting terribly; but as he now knew
that it was indeed Paul whom he had seen, he continued to run.

After gaining considerably on the trio, however,
Benny suddenly stopped, for he noticed that one
of the three carried a pistol. What could it mean?
Could it be?—why, yes, certainly; the man was one
of the deputy-sheriffs, and the man beside whom Paul
was walking — holding by one arm, in fact, as if he
were dragging him along—must be the prisoner.

PAUL AND THE COUNTERFEITER.

Benny was no longer afraid. Paul, he was sure, could protect him against at least six desperate criminals if necessary, even without the help of a deputy-sheriff with a pistol. "Mister," gasped Benny, as he overtook the officer, who walked a little in the rear of the others, "did — Paul — oh, my! — did Paul—catch the—the prisoner?"

"No, Benny, no," exclaimed Paul, who had looked backward on hearing Benny's voice; "I hadn't anything to do with catching him."

"He would have done it, though; I'll bet a hundred to one he would," said the deputy, "if he had met him before I did. I don't believe that boy knows what it is to be afraid."

"Of course he doesn't," said Benny, proudly.

"Benny," said Paul, "come around here by me; don't be afraid."

Benny obeyed, though rather fearfully, for the prisoner, with his face rather dirty, and bleeding besides, was not an assuring object to be only a boy's width away from.

"Benny," said Paul, "don't you go to telling the boys that I had any share in catching — in catching this man. You know how such stories get about if there's the slightest excuse for them."

"I won't," said Benny; "but I can tell that you helped bring him in, can't I? because you're doing it, you know."

"Don't say that either," Paul replied. "I'm not helping at all — not to bring him in, that is. The man is very tired; he's been in the woods all night, lying on the ground, and he's had no break- fast; he is weak, and I'm helping him, not the sheriff. Don't you see how the poor fellow leans against me?"

"Yes," said Benny. Then he dropped his voice to a whisper and said, "Would you mind telling him that I'm sorry for him too, even if he did—"

"Tell him yourself," said Paul, quickly. "And go on the other side of him and give him a lift."

Benny obeyed the last half of Paul's instructions, but the strangeness of his position made him entirely

forget the first part, and he was wicked enough to
wish that, as they reached the more thickly settled
part of the town, people who saw them might think,
if only for an hour or two, that he and Paul, two
boys, had caught the dreadful counterfeiter. And
his wish was gratified even more than he had dared
to hope, for suddenly they came face to face with
Ned Johnston, who gave them just one wondering
look, and then flew about town and told every boy
that the prisoner had been caught, and that Paul
and Benny did it.

Arrived at the jail, the deputy pointed with his
pistol to the still open door.

"One moment, please," said the prisoner. "Boys,
I am very much obliged to you. Will you shake
hands?"

He put out his hand toward Benny as he spoke,
and Benny took it; then he gave a hand to Paul,
and Paul looked him straight in the face so long
that Benny was sure he was going to make certain
of the man's looks in case he ever broke loose again

and had to be followed. Then the man went into his cell, and Paul stood by until he saw the three great bolts securely shot, after which he and Benny went together toward their homes.

CHAPTER XI.

THE TRIAL.

"WHAT do you think was the counterfeiter's excuse for running away?" asked Sam Wardwell of Canning Forbes, on meeting him at the Post-office, to which both boys had been sent by their parents.

"I give it up," said Canning, who had not the slightest taste for guessing.

"He said he would have come back and given himself up after court had met and adjourned, but he didn't want to be tried now."

"He wanted to wait for some new evidence in his defence, perhaps," suggested Canning.

"New grandfather!" ejaculated Sam, very contemptuously. "He wanted to stay in jail here, doing nothing, for the next six months, rather than

go to the Penitentiary and work hard. That's what
my father says."

"Perhaps your father is right," said Canning;
" but what does he think of Paul ?"

" What does he think?" answered Sam; "why,
just what everybody else thinks; he thinks Paul
is the greatest boy that ever was, and he says he
wishes I would be just like him."

" Well, why don't you ?" asked Canning.

" How can I ?" said Sam, in an aggrieved tone.
" I can't do just as I please, as Paul can, and I
haven't got any great mystery to keep me up, as
everybody knows Paul has."

" Didn't you ever have a great mystery?" asked
Canning.

" Never but once," said Sam; "that was when I
hooked a big package of loaf-sugar out of father's
store, and had to keep finding new places to hide
it in until it was eaten up."

" I suppose that mystery helped keep you up?"
suggested Canning.

" Well, you see— Oh, look ! there comes father;
I suppose he's wondering why I don't bring his letters. Good-bye;" and Sam got away from that very
provoking question as fast as possible.

As for the other boys, they simply sat on the
sidewalk opposite old Mrs. Bartle's, and worshipped
the house from which their hero had not been successfully coaxed to come out. In spite of Paul's
caution to Benny, and the promises that were made
in return, the deputy had talked so enthusiastically
about Paul to all the men he met, that the story
sped about town that Paul had done as much toward recapturing the prisoner as the officer had.
This story might have been spoiled had Benny acted
according to the spirit of his promise, but the little
fellow had been so elated by the looks that people
gave him, as he marched with Paul and the counterfeiter through the street, that he could not bear
to deliberately rob himself of his fame, as of course
he would do as soon as Paul's story had been told.
So Benny refused to be seen; he went to bed very

10

early, and before breakfast he had hidden himself
in the unused attic of his mother's cottage, where he
nursed his glory until he felt that he was simply
starving for something to eat.

And all this while his fictitious valor was nowhere in the eyes of the populace, for Mr. Morton
himself had gone out immediately after breakfast,
and had himself given Paul's version of the affair
to every one, besides giving Benny a fair share of
the credit for the tender-heartedness displayed by
the two boys toward the captive, so that when Benny finally entered the world again he found he had
lost some hours of praise to which he was honestly
entitled. As for Paul, the teacher begged every
one to say nothing at all to him about it. The
boy was somewhat peculiar, he said; the affair had
made a very painful impression upon him, and any
one who really admired him could best prove it by
treating him just as before, and not reminding him
in any way of Laketon's most famous day.

Mr. Morton had not yet decided whether to open

his school again, and the boys, although they would
have been sorry to have him go away from Laketon, hoped he would not decide before court opened,
for now that the counterfeiter had been mixed up
in some way with two of their own number, the
boys with one accord determined that they would
have to attend the trial; indeed, it seemed to some
of them that the trial could not go on without
them, for did they not know the two boys who had
helped bring the prisoner back from the woods?
They thought they did.

When the day for the trial came, and the sheriff
opened the court-room, the doors of which had been
kept locked because of the immense crowd that
threatened to fill the house in advance of the hour
for the session, he was surprised to find seventeen
boys in the front seats of the gallery. On questioning them, he learned that most of them had entered
through a window before sunrise, and that two had
slept in the gallery all night. He was about to
remove the entire party, but the boys begged so

hard to be allowed to remain, and they reminded him so earnestly that they all were particular friends of Paul, that the sheriff, who once had been a boy himself, relented, and let them remain.

It was about six in the afternoon, according to the boys, but only a quarter before ten by the court-house clock, when the front doors were opened and the crowd poured in. Within the next five minutes any boy in that front gallery row could have sold his seat for a dollar, but not a boy flinched from what he considered a public duty, although every one knew just what to do with a dollar if he could get it. Soon the lawyers flocked in by the judge's door, and grouped themselves about the table inside the rail, and at five minutes before ten his honor the judge entered and took his seat. Then the sheriff allowed Mr. Morton and Paul to enter by the judge's door, because they were unable to get through the crowd in front. At sight of Paul the whole front row of the gallery burst into a storm of hand-clapping.

THE SHERIFF ENFORCES ORDER.

The judge rapped vigorously with his little mallet, and exclaimed, "Mr. Sheriff, preserve order. The court is now open."

The sheriff, first giving chairs in the lawyers' circle to Paul and the teacher, because there were no other seats vacant, went down in front of the gallery, and shouted to the boys that if they made any more disturbance he would throw them all out of the window and break their heads on the pavement below.

No lighter threat would have been of any avail, for a more restless set of boys than they were during the next half-hour never was seen. It seemed to them that the trial never would begin; the lawyers talked to the judge about all sorts of things, and the judge looked over papers as leisurely as if time were eternity; but finally his honor said,

"Mr. Sheriff, bring in John Doe."

Every one in the front row of the gallery stood up, two or three minutes later, as Ned Johnston, who sat where he could look through the open door by which the judge had entered, signalled that the prisoner was coming. Many other people stood up when the sheriff and the prisoner entered, for all were curious to have a good look at the man whom but few of them had seen. The sheriff placed John Doe in the prisoners' box, where, to the great disgust of the boys, only the back of a head and two shoulders could be seen from the gallery. His honor nodded at the clerk, and the clerk arose, cleared his throat, and said,

"John Doe, stand up."

The prisoner obeyed; and as his head was slightly turned, so as to face the clerk, the boys had a fair view of it. It did not seem a bad face; indeed, it was rather handsome and pleasing, although there was a steady twitching of the lips that prevented its looking exactly the same from first to last.

"John Doe," said the clerk, turning over some of the sheets of a very bulky document he held in his hand, "a Grand-jury appointed by this Court has found a true bill of indictment against you for

.passing counterfeit money, to wit, a five-dollar note
purporting to have been issued by the Founders'
National Bank of Mechanics' Valley, State of Penn-
sylvania, the same note having been offered in pay-
ment for goods purchased from Samuel Wardwell,
a merchant doing business in this town of Laketon,
and for passing similar bills upon other persons
herein resident. Are you guilty or not guilty?"

"Guilty!" answered the prisoner.

A sensation ran through the house, and at least
half a dozen of the fifty or more citizens who had
hoped to be drawn on the jury whispered to their
neighbors that it was a shameful trick to appeal to
the judge's sympathy, and get off with a light sentence; but they hoped that his honor would not
be taken in by any such hypocritical nonsense.

"John Doe," said his honor, solemnly, "I have
been informed by an old acquaintance of yours of
your entire history. You are well born and well
bred; you had promising prospects in life, and a
family that you should have been proud of. But

you gambled; you fell from bad to worse; and a bullet aimed at you by an officer of the law, in the discharge of his duty, struck and killed your loving, suffering wife. Such of your family as remains to you would honor any one, even the highest man in the land, and I am assured that you are sincerely desirous of forsaking evil courses and devoting your life to this — family. Old friends, classmates of yours, who are held in high respect wherever they are known, are ready and willing to assist you to regain your lost manhood; so, in consideration of your plea, your professions of penitence, and the responsibilities which your misdeeds have increased instead of lessened, I sentence you to confinement in the county jail for the shortest period allowed by the law covering your offence, to wit, six months. Sheriff, remove the prisoner."

The prisoner bowed to the judge, and then looked toward Mr. Morton and Paul. He tried hard to preserve his composure as the sheriff led him through the lawyers' circle and toward the judge's door, but

"FATHER!"

somehow his eyes filled with tears. Perhaps this was the reason that Paul, in spite of Mr. Morton's hand on his arm, sprung from his chair, threw his arms around the prisoner's neck, and exclaimed,

"Father!"

CHAPTER XII.

THE END OF IT.

O Paul Grayson's secret was out at last, and now the boys wished there never had been any secret at all.

"I've had lots of fun trying to puzzle it out," said Ned Johnston to Napoleon Nott on the afternoon of the day of the trial, "but now I wish that I hadn't. Think of poor Paul!"

"I wish he had been a prince in exile," said Napoleon Nott, "for then he wouldn't have had a chance to tell on himself. Princes' sons never have their fathers tried for passing counterfeit money. But I'll tell you what; the way that Paul looked when he said 'Father!' that day was just like a picture in a book I've got, named 'Doomed to Death; or, the

Pirate's Protégé.' I'll bring it to school some day and show it to you all."

"I'll break every bone in your body if you do," said Will Palmer.

Notty suddenly remembered that his mother had sent him to the market to order something, so he hurried away from society that he had mistakenly supposed might be congenial, while Ned Johnston made the round of the residences of the various boys who had been at school with Paul. The end of it all was that the entire school met in the school-yard that evening after supper for the purpose of formally drafting resolutions of sympathy. Condolence also was suggested by Sam Wardwell, but Canning Forbes said that the meeting should not make a fool of itself if he could prevent it.

If the roll of Mr. Morton's school had been called that evening at that meeting, not a single absentee would have been reported. Even Charlie Gunter, who had begun half an hour before to shake with a chill, was present; and although his remarks were somewhat jerky, and his sentences bitten all to pieces by his chattering teeth, he spoke so feelingly that no one manifested the slightest inclination to laugh.

It had been intended that the meeting should be organized in as grand style as any town-meeting to consider the dog-tax question had ever been, but somehow there was a general unloosening of tongues, and no one thought to move that the assemblage should be called to order.

"It's easy enough now to see why Paul played so splendidly in that tableau of 'Civilization,'" said Will Palmer.

"Yes, indeed, it is," said Canning Forbes; "and easy, too, to understand why he fought so hard against taking the part when every one asked him to do it."

"No wonder he wasn't afraid to walk beside the prisoner after the deputy-sheriff had captured him," said Sam Wardwell. "I don't believe I'd have been afraid myself, if my father had been the counterfeiter. And say, Mr. Morton came into the store

THE MEETING IN THE SCHOOL-YARD.

this morning and offered father a five-dollar bill to make up his loss by the bad bill that Paul's father passed on him, and what do you think father said?"

"We give it up," said Canning Forbes, quickly. "Tell us what it was."

"Why," Sam answered, "he said that he wouldn't touch it for a thousand dollars, and if ever the prisoner needed money or anything during his six months, all he needed to do was to send to him. Father was telling mother about the whole thing last night when I went home, and when I went in he jumped up and hugged me and kissed me. He hasn't done that before since I was a little boy."

"Now I know why Paul used to forget his game and stare at the jail windows so hard," said Benny Mallow.

"Ye-es," chattered Charlie Gunter, "and why he—he was al-always wh-wh-wh-whistling when he passed the jail."

"And why he never could be happy unless a game of ball was going on in the lot by the jail," resumed

Benny. "If I'd only known all about it, I would have sweated to death on the hottest day of the summer rather than not have obliged him."

"Some of the girls thought it was very unmanner-ly for Paul to have been the first to leave Benny's party the night of the escape," said Will Palmer. "I'm going to call specially on each one of those girls and make her take it back."

"And if either of them refuses," said Sam Ward-well, "just you tell me. She sha'n't ever eat an-other philopena with me while she lives; not if she lives for a thousand years."

"He begged me to tell all of you boys that he hadn't anything to do with the catching of the pris-oner," confessed Benny, for the first time. "I wish I'd gone and done it right away! Oh dear; I do think I'm the very wickedest boy that ever lived—except Cain."

"I wonder who told the judge so much about Paul's father?" asked Ned Johnston.

"Why, Mr. Morton, of course," replied Canning

Forbes. "Haven't you seen through that yet? Mr. Morton told in school one day, you know, that Paul was the son of an old friend of his."

At least half of the boys had not put the two ends of this thread together before, but they all admitted that Canning had done it correctly.

"Certainly," said Will Palmer, "and that explains why Mr. Morton was so frequent in his visits to the prison."

"Yes, and why Paul felt so dreadful after *he* had been there the first time," said Benny. "It just used him up completely; you'd hardly have thought him the same boy."

Mention of that incident recalled to the boys the manner in which Paul had come to go to the prison, so one after another looked at Joe Appleby, who had not yet said a word, but Joe did not seem angry; on the contrary, he said,

"Boys, of course I didn't know how what I said was affecting Paul, but I know now, and I'm going to apologize to him the first chance I get. I'm going

to ask him to forgive me, or to take it out of me, if
he'd rather; and," continued Joe, after a short pause,
" I'm not going to wait for the chance, but I'm going
to make it."

"Hurrah for Appleby !" shouted Will Palmer, and
as three cheers were given Will crossed over to the
big boy of whom he had long been jealous, and
shook hands with him, and all the other boys understood it; so when Canning Forbes cried, "Three
cheers for Palmer !" they too were given with a will.

"I want to make a suggestion," said Canning
Forbes, when the cheering had ended. "We came
here to adopt resolutions for Paul Grayson, but I'm
sure he'd be better pleased if we would say nothing
about the matter; any reference to it would be certain to give him pain. The best we can do is to
treat him with special kindness hereafter, if he stays,
and never, by any word or deed, make reference to
the past. If there is any one who insists on resolutions, let him adopt them for himself and about
himself. In spite of having had a father who was

a gambler and a criminal, Paul is the most sensible, honest, honorable, pleasant fellow in this town. Let each one of us make a resolution that if a boy can become what Paul is, in spite of such dreadful trouble, those of us who have honest fathers and happy homes ought to do at least as well."

" I'll do that," said Benny Mallow, " right straight away, and I'll write it down in a book as soon as I get home, so as to be sure never to forget it."

" So will I," said Napoleon Nott. " I'll write it on the first page of ' The Exiled Prince,' so I'll be sure to see it often."

Such of the boys as did not agree verbally to Canning's suggestion seemed to be making the resolution quietly, and the meeting soon broke up. As Benny started for home it suddenly occurred to him that, now the secret was out, Paul might go away; he certainly would if Mr. Morton did not open school.

This was too dreadful an uncertainty to be endured, so Benny hurried to old Mrs. Bartle's and asked to see the teacher. Mr. Morton quickly quieted·his mind by saying that the school would continue for at least the half-year that Paul's father remained in the jail. Of course Paul would be one of the class; indeed, Mr. Morton was willing that Benny should tell every one that the only reason he had opened school at Laketon at all was his desire to be near the old friend whom he could not desert in his trouble, and to have near the prisoner, whose real name was Paul Gray, the son for whom, since the death of his wife, Paul Gray had felt an affection that Mr. Morton knew would make a good man of him when again he had a chance to start in the world.

When Paul Gray's term of imprisonment expired he and Paul went away together, and no one was so unmannerly as to ask them where they were going. Some of the people of the town talked of taking up a subscription for the unfortunate man, but Mr. Morton said it would not be necessary, as Gray's old friends had arranged to start him in business. All of the boys were as sorry to part with Paul as if the boy had been going to his grave, particularly because Canning Forbes had reminded them that it would not do to ask him to write to them, because his father would prefer that no one who had known his old history should know where he began his new life.

But every one begged Paul's picture, which pleased Paul greatly; and after a supper given expressly in Paul's honor by Joe Appleby, Canning Forbes arose and presented Paul an album containing the portraits of all the members of the old class. The pictures were not remarkably good, having been done by a carpenter who sometimes took "tin-types" merely to oblige people, he said, but the album was handsome, having been ordered from New York, regardless of expense, by Sam Wardwell's father, and on the cover was the inscription, in gold letters, " Don't forget us, for we can't forget you."

THE END.

www.ingramcontent.com/pod-product-compliance
Lightning Source LLC
Chambersburg PA
CBHW020013030726
47500CB00002B/570